MW01257963

The Shattered Dreams

The Shattered Dreams

Gita Zikherman-Greisdorf

THE SHATTERED DREAMS

iUniverse books may be ordered through booksellers or by contacting:

iUniverse
1663 Liberty Drive
Bloomington, IN 47403
www.iuniverse.com
1-800-Authors (1-800-288-4677)

ISBN: 978-1-5320-1941-8 (sc)
ISBN: 978-1-5320-1940-1 (e)

Library of Congress Control Number: 2017903687

Print information available on the last page.

iUniverse rev. date: 06/14/2017

No more happy days,
the concert was not played,
the beloved people were killed,
the golden childhood finished in one day,
June 22, 1941.

Endorsements

It was very enlightening to read something so personal and honest. This book isn't just a story that I can't even imagine, but one of remembrance, knowledge and emotion.
I can't wait for her next book.

- Jane Trembour

Thank you for sharing your book with me. What you saw and what you lived through is incredible. I am very impressed with your writing, and you as a person. Thank you again for allowing me to read this. I will remember it and share it.

- Chris Hackman

Gita, your story is one that must be read, remembered and shared. Your memories and attention to detail are just amazing. Thank you for writing this and sharing it with me. We must never forget this time in history.

- Lauren Greenfield

Acknowledgement

Thank you to my dear parents, who gave me love, respect and support throughout their whole lives. They taught me to treat all people in the same way.

I want to thank my family – my son Jacob, my daughter Luba, and my daughter-in-law Robin, and my grandchildren for supporting me.

Special thanks to Lauren for putting up with me in my work.

Introduction

Coming to America was a huge change in our lives. It affected our views on life, our values, and made us question what we knew of right and wrong. As a parent of a son and daughter, I felt that it was my job to teach them the right way of going through life. Things like working hard to achieve your dreams and meet your goals. These will not be served to you on a silver platter.

Then it suddenly dawned on me- my children don't know anything about my childhood. They know nothing of where I came from, what kind of life I had during the war, and most of all, how our family survived the Holocaust.

It was then I got the urge to sit down and write. The words poured out of me without even having to think about it. My whole life spilled onto the paper. Before I knew it, I had a manuscript.

I would like my story to be read and shared by all generations. I want my readers to know the story of what happened when Hitler came to power, and what happened to the Jewish people during this time. I want young people to know the atrocities that came from bigotry and hatred, so it will never be repeated.

On a lighter note, I would like my book to not only be informative, but entertaining as well. It shows what life was like in Russian Collective farms with humor and honesty.

I believe this unique story will touch readers of all ages.

Chapter 1

My Parents

Rachmiel & Eugenia Zikherman

I remember my childhood very clearly. All the events pass through my mind like they happened yesterday.

I was a very skinny little girl with big golden curls hanging around my face—a Shirley Temple type. I would sing and dance like she did too. She was my hero. I was the youngest child in a large, extended family. My mother had three sisters and two brothers, and my father had one brother and one sister. Both sets of their parents were alive and well during this time.

I was everyone's buddy. I was the child everyone loved to babysit. I was treated with much love and respect. I was an entertainer, always singing and dancing for everyone to watch and applaud. I knew all the songs my mom and her sisters liked to sing, and my parents would sing and dance with us too. When company arrived, my father played the mandolin or the banjo. He was a very talented man who taught himself how to play.

I was a very inquisitive child. I wanted to participate in everything. Once a circus came parading through our city streets, with music and clowns on stilts. I was so amused, that I started following the parade, not paying any attention to where I was going! It brought me away from my home, to the outskirts of town. There I saw a huge round tent, closed on all sides. I followed the clowns inside. I was mesmerized at what my five year old eyes saw- a circus! I have never seen anything like it before.

Meanwhile at my house, my mom noticed I wasn't playing outside where she thought I was. She became alarmed and went looking for me. She asked around, and no one had seen me. She ran home to tell my father that I was missing. He dropped what he was doing and ran outside. He went towards the park, asking everyone he passed if they have seen a little curly haired girl in a red polka dot dress, but no one had.

After three or four hours of searching, my father found a man who said he saw a girl of that description at the circus. He ran to the circus, didn't buy a ticket, and just ran into the tent. He was stopped by circus employees. But he explained the situation, and they showed him where I was right away. I was by the side of the arena with the clowns. They all knew me by then, and if my dad hadn't found me, I probably would have been taken away with them! My dad ran over and took me in his arms, almost crying. He was so happy. He kissed and hugged me all the way home. He and my mom explained to me that is was a very dangerous thing I did, and that i should never wander off without my parents again.

My father's parents were poor and could not give him an education. My grandfather started his career installing the glass in windows and doors at thirteen years old. He barely made a living, yet he had to support two sons, a daughter, and his wife.

When my father was thirteen years old, my grandfather told him that he could not support him anymore and he would have to start working. So my dad went to a tailor shop and learned the trade, and that was what he was all his life.

Even though my dad lacked a formal education, he was a very smart man. He taught himself to read and read books about everything. He wanted to learn as much as possible and hoped to fulfill his dreams of giving his children the education he never had.

He became a very good tailor and opened up a tailor shop in the front room of our apartment. He had three young men working for him, and he was making a nice living. Every summer, he would rent a cottage in Pogulyanka, on a resort for our family. We would pack up the horse-drawn carriage and make our way to a little village where the cottage was located.

The cottage was a two-room house in a clearing with two other cottages nearby. On one side of the cottage was a cornfield with beautiful blue cornflowers and daisies. I loved to pick the flowers. I would put half in a vase and with the other half, my mom taught me how to make a wreath to wear on my head. On the other side was a pine forest, where my mom would put up hammocks for us to sleep in after lunch. There was a riverbank and a lake nearby for us to swim in.

In the mornings, a man in a carriage would come by. He would yell out, "Fresh cottage cheese! Fresh milk! Smoked fish! Fresh rolls!" It was all delicious, and everyone would run out and buy whatever they needed. In the evenings, my mom would take us to one of the farmer's yards. We would wait for the cows to come back from the pasture, and the farmer's wife would milk them and give us the warm, fresh milk. It was considered very healthy, and I loved it.

At the summer cottage
Left to right – my mom, her cousin,
her sister Dora, and me as a little girl

My dad worked all week in the city. Every Friday afternoon, he came out to the cottage by bus, and we would all go to meet him. It was like a big holiday when he arrived.

On Saturdays, my mom and dad liked to take us deep into the woods to pick berries and mushrooms. My mom would pack a lunch, and we would go for the whole day. We would bring home baskets full of blueberries, raspberries, strawberries, and mushrooms.

We spent about three months at the resort, and I loved it. I loved the time when we were going to the cottage, and I loved the time we had to go home too. In later years, when I was taking music lessons, my dad bought an old motorcycle and would come to the cottage three times a week to take me to my lessons.

Chapter 2

Nothing Is Forever

My father loved music more than anything, and he wanted his little girl to become a pianist. When I was five, he took me to a young pianist at the local banquet hall to assess my musical talent. Her name was Haya Gafanovitch. She looked down skeptically at me, played a few tunes, and told me to sing them. I sang my heart out for her. She was very impressed and played a few more complicated tunes. I sang those too. She was very amused and decided to accept me as a student.

My father was overwhelmed with happiness. His dream was coming true. Soon after, he took the small amount of money he had saved and bought me an old, out-of-tune piano. It was a real jalopy, as I called it. Half of the keys were sunken in, but I was happy to have it. I played and played my first pieces of music.

My father could not stand listening to the sounds of that old, out-of-tune piano. He soon decided to sell it and bought another piano. This one was old and grand.

It was so huge and long that it took up our whole dining room. It sounded good and lasted for three years.

I was going to the banquet hall for my lessons three times a week. It was winter and the hall was not heated, so in the corner of the stage where the piano was standing, my teacher lit a little wood-burning stove. It gave off a little warmth, and my hands did not freeze so badly. I remember once I had a new winter coat that my father had another tailor make up for me. I had my new coat on, and my teacher wanted to explain something to me before I left. I happened to be standing very close to the oven, and I smelled something burning. I turned around, and my coat was smoking! I was horrified. It burned a big hole on the bottom of my new coat. I went home crying, thinking that I could not show it to my father. I came in holding my music books awkwardly to cover the hole. I managed to hide it for a few months, until my mom noticed that I was always walking sideways. I sadly showed her what had happened. She told my father. He hugged me and said that he would never punish me for my misfortune. He fixed my coat so well the hole was almost invisible. I was so happy.

In the spring, after five months of my studying with Haya, she told my father that I needed a more advanced teacher. She said that she was not good enough for me and recommended me to the best music teacher in town—Madam Gutovska. She was a German woman who lived with her daughter, Nina. Nina was a very good violinist. I was very excited to meet with my new teacher. She lived in a very nice apartment. This was a wonderful change from being in the huge, cold banquet hall I was used to. Madam Gutovska was very friendly but wanted to assess my talent before she decided to take me as her student. She asked me to play a few pieces from Bach. I was happy about that because I knew Bach very well and knew those pieces by heart.

After I finished, she told me that my first lesson would be in two days. That day came, and we began a beautiful relationship. I dearly loved her, and she loved me too. Every lesson for me was like a big holiday. It was not only the music; she also taught me about life. She taught me good manners, the history of music, and how to play in four hands. She gave me an education. Her daughter, Nina, and I put on concerts together. She played the violin, and I played the piano. I was so happy in my beautiful, carefree, worry-free world.

Two and a half years into my studies with Madam Gutovska, there came a day when I went into the apartment for my lesson and saw Madam Gutovska sobbing. She hugged me tightly, sat me down on the couch, and told me that she had very, very bad news. She informed me that she could no longer teach me. I was completely shocked and could not understand what I had done wrong or why this was happening. She started to explain things to me, and I slowly began to understand. She was talking about a man named Adolf Hitler. She said, "He's a man who commands all the German people of Europe to migrate back to Germany, and if they don't, they will be badly punished as traitors against Germany."

Madam Gutovska sounded very frightened and so upset. She didn't want to go. She hated the place where she was born. She loved our city, Daugavpils. It was not very big. It had about 115,000 people, and the population was very diverse. We had Latvians, Poles, Russians, Germans, and Jews. She had no idea exactly what was awaiting her in the "Fatherland," as Hitler described Germany.

At that time, Daugavpils was a culturally advanced city. We had a main transit railroad port, two movie theaters, a live theater, about forty synagogues and churches, and a conservatory. The Jews of Daugavpils were hardworking people. They owned small businesses, such as groceries, shoe-repair shops, tailor shops, bakeries, and a lot of domestic services. The location of our city was very convenient in all aspects. It was on the river Daugava which was a water way through White Russia, we had a lot of small lakes full of all kinds of fish and a lot of pine tree forests full of mushrooms and all kind of berries. This was a big help for poor people, that provided food and some money. They would bring the goods from the lakes and forests to the market and sell it. Everyone lived in peace and harmony.

In 1940, Latvia was occupied by the Soviet government peacefully. Since I was a small child at the time, I did not understand what was going on in the political world. To me, it was all fun. I would sing and play with the soldiers. They were all very nice.

After our conversation, Madam Gutovska told me that I must apply to the conservatory right away. She said, "One day, you will make me proud that I was your teacher." She believed in me as much as my father did.

One needed to apply and pass an exam in order to become a music student there. We decided then this was what I was going to do.

Meanwhile, my father was still saving money to buy a brand-new piano for me. He eventually sold the "coffin", as I called it. He ordered an upright "August Forster", a really great brand name. The new piano was to arrive in two weeks. Where would I practice during this time? My father asked a rich merchant whom we got cloth from if I could play at his home. He had three boys, and one was playing piano. They allowed me to come for an hour every day, but the time was always when the little one in the house was sleeping. I had to turn the sound off on the piano so I couldn't hear anything! But the practice was still good for my technique. I was preparing myself for the exam at the conservatory. The older son was practicing too, as his parents wanted him to play at the conservatory as well. Madam Gutovska prepared me well for the exam.

I was eight years old when the big day finally arrived. To be accepted into the conservatory was no ordinary thing, especially for a little girl like me with a father who was just a tailor. It was meant for the rich children.

I sat down at the piano, and I suddenly forgot everything I knew! I felt as if I were in a dream. I realized when I finished playing, I had played beautifully! After the exams ended, the teacher came out and called the names of the students who had been accepted. My name was among the first few to be called! I was ecstatic! My father and my beloved teacher would be so proud and happy. (By the way, the merchant's son didn't pass and they were very upset.)

Going to the conservatory was the best time for me. I had an excellent teacher. My teacher's name was Mrs. Volpert-Rabinovich. She always expected perfection from me, and she was very strict. If I made a mistake, she slapped me on my fingers. Gradually things started to get out of hand. She was always in a bad mood, and I became afraid of her. This caused me to fumble my notes and get in more trouble. It turned out that she had problems at home and was letting out her misery on my poor little hands. One day, she hit me so badly that I started to cry and left the classroom. I went to see the principal, whom I'd never seen in my life. I was very frightened, but I needed help. I badly wanted to be a good pianist. In the lobby, I met a very tall man who was extremely distinguished looking. He bent down to me and asked me why I was crying. I started to cry even harder and then slowed down and began to speak. He couldn't understand me. He picked me up in his arms and brought me to a big study. We sat on a big couch, and he asked me to tell him my troubles. It was then that I realized that this man was the principal. I felt very comfortable and secure with him. I told him everything about that teacher. I told him how she punished me for making mistakes and how I was very afraid of her.

The principal's name was Yanis Kruminsh. He promised me that this would never happen again and that I didn't have to be afraid anymore. He told me to return to the teacher. I came out of his study feeling very brave and confident. I had his power on my side.

On that day, I promised myself that I would be the best pianist in the conservatory and nobody would ever touch me again. I was good, very good. My teacher was called into the principal's office about her bad behavior. From then on, she was nice to me. She wanted me to become a perfect player and predicted that I would be a great pianist.

One day, she brought me a big music book. It was Beethoven. She showed me a piece of music that I would play in my first concert, which was supposed to be in September 1941. The best students would participate in this concert, and it was a big honor. I was nine years old at the time and very proud. I had five months to prepare for my concert. It was a very big job, very complicated. For hours, I would sit at the piano going through complicated pieces of music. It was hard to resist running out onto the street to play with my friends. They would always come to our windows and call me to come out and play, but I was determined to be the best and practicing lots of hours was the only way to do that.

I was my father's pride. He always told me that I was smart, good, witty, and very talented. Nobody ever yelled at me or showed me an unfriendly face. All my family loved me very much.

Chapter 3

My First Encounter with Hate

My grandparents on my mom's side lived four blocks from us. I visited them a few times a week. This was a big event for me. I was walking by myself, all dressed up. My grandma was an angel. Her name was Malka, which in Hebrew means "queen."

She always looked out the window to see if I was coming. When she saw me, she commanded her younger son, my uncle Sheil, "Sheil, the clever girl is coming. Run to the bakery and buy a fresh challah!"

My grandparents had their difficulties making a living. My grandfather was working at the train station, dispatching goods coming and going for stores and factories. For that time, he was educated, but he still had three daughters and two sons at home, and his salary was not enough.

I was a very bad eater, and Grandma always tried to feed me. My favorite meal was fresh challah with sweet tea. I would dip the challah in the tea, and it was the best meal for me. When I was playing outside with the children, she would run after me with a sandwich, looking for an opportunity to put a bite in my mouth.

My other grandmother had nine grandchildren, so she could not afford to feed everybody. They were never all there together, maybe three at one time, who were closer to my age. All of them were poor. My father was the most successful of her three children. When the children got hungry, she would give them black bread with sugar on top. To me, this looked very delicious. But, she would say to me "go home to eat, you have better things to eat". This was upsetting to me, because I wanted what the other children were eating. My grandmother loved me very much, maybe more than the other grandchildren, so she wanted me to have better things to eat. Every Saturday morning she invited me to her house for breakfast. She made coffee from acorns, which was brewing from Friday evening to Saturday morning in the big oven. I loved it very much.

I especially loved the Shabbat dinners and the holidays. I always visited both sets of my grandparents in the synagogue. They showed me off to the congregation and had me read the prayers, which I did very well. They would pray in response to me, and my grandparents were shining with pride. I loved both of my grandparents dearly.

My father's family
On the right is me next to my mom and behind her is
my father. Next to my mom is my grandmother, Sara-
Luba, with my little brother Samuil on her lap. Next to her
is my grandfather, Avraham and the rest of his family.

The bride is Dora, my mom's sister
in front of the bride is Gita in white dress, to the left
of Dora are Gita's grandparents - Avraham and Malka
Barkin, behind the bride is my uncle Haim Barkin.

Both of my grandparents lived in apartments with big courtyards. I would play with the neighbors' children at both homes, and I liked to play with all of them. There was a Latvian family I will remember to the end of my life. They had two girls, Betty and Erica. The father was a policeman. His name was Willis. I forgot his last name, but he was a real Nazi. He hated all the Jewish children and all the Jews, but for me, I felt he had a special hatred. He came home early one day while we were still playing. He ordered them to go home. He came up to me with a face full of rage and hatred and said, "You, Jew, go home, and never come close to my children!"

I felt like he wanted to kill me with his bare hands, and he would always pinch me very hard on my arm. I was terrified of him. He probably knew that the Germans would invade soon, and he was just waiting for them to arrive so he could come to our apartment and kill all of us. This was exactly what happened, but thank G-d we ran away before he came. He ransacked our home and took all our clothing, our furniture, my piano, and all of our belongings. We found this out after the war from the people who witnessed it.

So this was my golden childhood, which was finished on one day, June 22, 1941. The war had started. There were no more happy days, I did not play my concert, and beloved people were lost forever.

Chapter 4

The Beginning of War

That morning, my grandma came to our house. She was distraught. She and my mother were both crying.

"Mom! Grandma! Why are you crying?" I asked.

"It is a war, my child! It is a war!"

"But why are you crying?" I asked. "It will be so interesting! We will watch the men fighting on the streets through the windows. It will be fun!" I was nine and a half years old; what did I know about war? I knew only from fairy tales my mom had read to me. My mom and grandma hugged each other in bitter mourning. It was as if this was their last hug and they would never see each other again.

Daugavpils was close to Lithuania which was bordered with Poland. Poland was already occupied by the Germans. People were flooding to our city. They were running from the Nazis, and they told horrible stories of what they were doing to the Jews. They told us the Nazis were hunting Jews like animals and putting them in concentration camps. And the famous Dr. Josef Mengele was doing all kinds of horrible, inhumane "tests" on the Jews.

Everybody was horrified by all the stories. The words "The Nazis are coming!" were on every adult's mind. It felt like this was the end of life. Soon after this, our city was bombarded. In the beginning, after every bomb exploded, I would run with other children to see the fire. We were very amused and not scared at all. After a few days, the sirens went off more often and the bombs fell more often. We were ordered to hide in the cellars under larger buildings and stay there. I still felt like we were having fun, lying on the cement floor in the basement of a three-story building. There were a lot of people with their children. It was so bizarre to me. Some people had brought bags, pillows, and blankets. I was watching it all with interest, especially when people were shaking and crying after every explosion. I did not understand the enormity of what was happening.

My father was mobilized in the city guard, patrolling the city. Everybody thought that the war would end right away, that the Russian army was strong and they would stop Hitler very quickly.

A week or more had gone by since the first bomb hit our city. My father was a manager at a tailor shop at this time. He had a full safe of money from the shop to take to the bank. He put the money in a briefcase to deposit in the bank, but the bank was closed. He thought the bank would reopen another day. He was mobilized at this point, and had to report to his watch duty. He saw a co-worker, and asked him to take the money to the bank for him. The man took the briefcase, but the bank never reopened. So this man was left with all the money, which he kept, and never told my father. My father was a very trusting man. He never thought something like this would ever happen.

After this episode, my father had to go to his watch duty on the city tower. When one morning, all of a sudden, he felt a strange quietness. He heard not one sound. He called out the names of the other guards, but there was no answer. He left the tower. When he reached the ground, he found not one person around. He was left alone. Everybody had fled the post. That was when it dawned on him: the Germans were close, and he had to run to save his family.

Chapter 5

Running for Our Lives

It was early morning when my father came into the basement where we were sleeping. In a very calm voice, not to cause panic, he announced, "Attention! The Germans are already at the outskirts of the city. Save yourself! Run to the railroad station." It was mostly women with children and old people. The men were all in the army. Everyone started to cry and panic, and then it got to me too.

We ran across the street to our apartment. My mom took a loaf of bread and some sugar. This was all we had. She grabbed her new dress and put it in her purse. She must have loved it very much. I took my new coat. We ran to my father's parents' apartment. It was close to ours. My father begged them to run with us, but they refused.

My grandfather said, "Where will we go? We are old people. We are no harm to anybody. Nobody will touch us. But you hurry up and run as fast as you can!"

We were all crying and hugging. It was very difficult to say good-bye forever. We started out running to the railroad station. The streets looked like a battlefield of personal belongings, open suitcases, and discarded clothes, shoes, toys, and so on. It looked like somebody had opened up all the windows in the houses and thrown everything out onto the streets. I was shaking and held on very tight to my father's hand. My brother, Samuil, was only five years old at this time and my mom was holding tightly on to his hand.

I could not understand why people would throw out their belongings, so I asked my father about it. He explained to me that people packed all of their belongings in a suitcase, and had to run for their lives. The suitcases were too heavy to run with, so they had to take whatever they could carry and the rest was left in the streets. People were running in different directions, not knowing where to go. A lot of them said that the passenger railroad station was not functioning, so my father turned around and we ran to the other side of the city to the cargo station. A lot of people were running beside us, hoping to escape death. When we got there, the rails were half empty. One cargo train was closer to us. Everybody was happy to go inside, helping each other climb into it. It was extremely difficult because it was very high and had no steps. After everybody was in, my father went to the locomotive to look for a driver to start the train, but there was no one to do it. He was devastated. It was a train full of women, children, and elderly people. Time was very short, and there was no driver. My father felt that it was his responsibility to save these people. He ran from train to train and to all the buildings to look for a driver, and a miracle happened. He found one hiding. He asked him to start the train, but he refused. He was not going to save those "Jews"; he would rather see them die. But my father could not accept this kind of an answer. He had to make the man drive! He started to look around to find another strong man. God was with us. He saw an officer with a gun, who probably was lost from his company, as the army was running very fast. They were not prepared for a war with Hitler, for his *blitzkrieg*. It was all very sudden.

My father called the officer and explained the situation, and soon the driver, at gunpoint, was brought to the locomotive and started the train. The train began to move away from the horror that was awaiting us if we didn't escape.

Our train was moving very slowly. We would stop when the German planes above were throwing bombs at us. Sometimes they would fly very low to kill as many people as possible with machine guns. We were lying on the floor in the cattle car, praying for the bombs to miss us. We did not have food or water for days, and it was a hot July. I was wearing a warm winter dress, which my mom put on me in the cellar. Thank God that my mom had the bread and sugar. She would secretly give us very tiny pieces. The other people were not so lucky.

At each stop, my father would run with a teakettle somebody gave him to find precious water for everybody.

Gita Zikherman-Greisdorf

The car was very crowded. Everyone was very close to each other. A very old man with a long white beard was lying next to me on the floor. My mom felt sorry for him, so she would give him bread with sugar to eat. Every time the bombs exploded, he would start to pray and a little stream of urine would run over the floor. One morning, I woke up and he was lying next to me, dead. I was numb. I did not understand what was happening. I had never seen a dead person before, and I was devastated. At the next stop, he was taken out and was left beside the railroad tracks. We could not bury him because the bombs were falling rapidly, and we did not have the tools to bury him. During the bombing, fire was everywhere. We would jump from the train to hide in the ditches, as it was a very long bombing. One day when the *Messerschmidts* (German airplanes) left after heavy bombarding, my father grabbed us to see if we were alive, and what we saw in this minute was a horrible scene. A few cattle cars were destroyed, and all over were pieces of human bodies, brains hanging from the ceiling, blood all over. Everyone was thinking, *It could be us.*

After fourteen days of running from death, we got out of the war zone. We escaped through the front line, and the train brought us deep into Russia, to a city called Kuibishev (today it is called Samara). We were twelve thousand miles away from home in a strange country. We knew no one and had no friends and no relatives. It was just me, my parents, and my little brother. We would have to start a new life, and it would not be easy. But we considered ourselves lucky; we had escaped death.

Unfortunately, my mom's family—her two brothers, two sisters, and parents—did not know about the train we used to escape. Her parents with one sister and one brother went by foot. They walked for a few days and came to a small town with a railroad station. They got into a train they thought would take them further toward the Russian border, but they were deceived. The train was operated by the native fascists who took them right back to the killers' hands in Daugavpils. They would all be killed.

In the first days of the occupation, all the older people were taken to jail and then shot. The Germans did not have any use for them.

The young people and the children were taken to the ghetto, which was an old fortress by the river. The first year, the stronger people were kept alive as workers.

The children were grabbed from the mothers' hands and killed in front of them in different manners. My mom's younger sister Golda, along with her new baby and her husband, were taken to the ghetto.

My mom's youngest sister Golda, who was killed
in the ghetto with her baby and husband.

The first thing the Nazis did was rip the baby from
her arms and hit him on a pole, holding him by his
little legs. When I think of it, I feel that there is no
punishment by God that can pay for such a heinous
crime.

Human beings do not do this to their children.
Animals don't do it to their kind. So who were these
monsters?

The first of May was a big holiday in Russia, similar to
America's Labor Day. The Nazis decided to celebrate

it differently on this particular day in 1942. They committed a huge mass killing of Jews. This was the day when my mother's sister, her husband, and his whole family were killed. My mom's brother, Chaim, tried to escape. He was in the ghetto with his fiancée. They decided to flee. They found a farmer who was delivering goods to the Germans. He agreed to hide them in his carriage, under the straw and boxes, to take them out of the ghetto. The day arrived. They had agreed to meet in a certain place. My uncle went to the meeting spot, but his fiancée was not there. He ran to look for her. He did not want to go without her. Meanwhile, she showed up while he was off looking for her. The farmer came, and she got into his carriage, and off they went. There was no time to wait for Chaim. People saw him running around, acting suspiciously. Someone alerted the guards to his behavior. The guards began looking for him. He realized this, so as soon as he heard the guards closing in on him, he ran into an outhouse and jumped into the sewer hole. The guards went in after him. They saw him in the sewer and shot him right then and there. This hole of human waste became his grave. He was only twenty years old.

Chapter 6

The Kolkhoz

We arrived in Kuybishev (now called Samara) The big cities could not accept refugees. They did not have enough housing or food. Everybody and everything was mobilized for the front. So the refugees were sent to the *kolkhoz*, collective farms, in small villages, where they could work in the fields and produce for themselves and the cities. Kolkhoz were villages that could be any size and could grow any type of crops. It all depended on their location. The members of the kolkhoz were assigned a small house, one cow (two cows if the family was larger), four to five sheep, one to two pigs, and chickens. Behind each house, every family had a space to plant whatever they wanted. Everybody had an assigned job on the farm. Members were paid by how many hours they worked. They were paid in money, grain, and whatever products they produced. They used the money to buy clothes from a clothing truck that came by a couple of times a month. There was also a store, called the village store, where they would sell all the household necessities, like salt, sugar, pepper, soap, and so on.

We were transported by a truck to our new home in a small kolkhoz. We were dropped off at the village's school. All the people of the village came there to see the refugees. They had never seen people from Western Europe, especially Jews. They were told, by their parents and grandparents, that Jews were the devil. They would scare the little children by telling them that if they did not behave, the Jews would come and take them away. None of them had ever seen a Jewish person before, so all came to witness the huge event.

They saw that we are not so scary looking. In fact, they realized we were just normal people. The children took me and my brother to play in the school yard. All the kids came up to us to touch our foreheads. I asked them, "Why are you doing that?"

They said, "To see the horns."

Their parents and grandparents had told them that Jewish people had horns. As soon as the inspection was done, we were accepted into their circle.

Russian people are good-hearted and hospitable. The people of this kolkhoz were no different. Everybody brought us something: a clay pot, a clay bowl, a spoon, and many other gifts to start our new life in this village. They did not have too much themselves, but these families took the refugees into their homes. Other housing options were not available in this small village.

These people's homes were very small—two rooms at the most, sometimes three, but that was very rare. The family who took us in had two rooms. They slept in the back one, and we slept in the front room on the floor. They made us a straw mattress and gave us two blankets. They were poor themselves, but still they shared their home and their food with us. We could never forget them.

My father went to work in the fields of the kolkhoz. My mother helped around the house. It was a hot summer in 1941. The drinking water was coming from a little river in the village. This was the same river where the people of this kolkhoz would swim, wash the laundry, and fish. They would also fill up buckets with water to take home to cook and drink. Usually the owner of the house would take an ox and buggy to the river, fill a big barrel with water, and bring it back to the house. This barrel of water would be enough for four to five days. If you wanted a drink, you had to take a special tin cup and get the water from the barrel. We were not used to this kind of water. It contained all kinds of insects and dirt. My whole family got dysentery, but I got a very serious case of it. My parents had to take me to the little hospital in our village. This was actually a small house with 3 smaller rooms, with two beds in each room. There were no doctors left there, only a few very good nurses. People were dying every day from dysentery. I was close to death as well, but the nurses took very good care of me. They watched over me day and night.

After two weeks of being very sick, I started to get better, although I was still frail and weak. After one more week, my father brought me home in his arms. He decided to look for a job in a larger village with better conditions. We soon moved fifteen miles away to a larger village.

Uniforms and warm clothing were needed for the army. Being that my father was a tailor, he organized a tailor shop in the village. He hired women who could sew by hand and work on sewing machines. If they did not know how to use the machines, he would teach them. They started making military clothing. We were placed at a larger house in the new village. We moved between four houses, but we still had to sleep on the floor in the first room. Life was very difficult. We did not have anything but a few clay bowls and four wooden spoons. We did not have a pillow to sleep on. My mom came up with an idea. There were a lot of geese living by the river, and there were many feathers along the banks. We went every day and collected every feather. In the evening, we took out the soft part of the feathers and threw out the hard parts. By winter, we had made four small pillows. We were rich! Now everybody had a pillow.

For the winter, Dad made us warm quilted jackets. The fabric was thin, but there was cotton insulation inside, so it was warm. For our feet, we made felt boots from lamb's wool. They went up to the knees. Bread and grain to cook a meal were rationed. The summer was better because there were vegetables. The best dinner was bread with melon, watermelon, or whatever fruit or vegetables we could get.

Chapter 7

Going to Tashkent, Uzbekistan

B ut winter was bad and very cold in the Kuibishev region. Our village name was Pestravka. Life in Pestravka was tough. We did not have enough clothes or food. The only food that was available came from the fields and gardens that the farmers planted and harvested. There was no food to buy, and no money. We were getting only grain that was given to us by the Russian government. My father had to take it to the mill to make flour. Then my mom would bake the bread for us. There was nothing else, so we suffered from hunger and cold.

So my father came up with the idea to move to a warmer place in Russia, to Uzbekistan, so we would not freeze so badly and life would be easier. But he forgot about what was going on, a terrible war, hunger, and diseases. He did not get enough information about what was going on in the warmer states. There were too many refugees. It was hot. There was hunger and typhus, which took so many lives every day, but he did not know this at the time, so the decision was made to go there.

My mom started to prepare toasted bread for the road. My dad earned frozen butter for all his work. My father also made us warmer clothes. It was January, the coldest time in that region. Temperatures dipped to 35 to 40 degrees below zero Celsius. In our village, there was no transportation at all—no trains, no trucks, and no roads, only dirt roads which were all covered in snow. There were only oxen for transportation. But in this extreme cold, an ox could freeze, so nobody was going anywhere this winter.

My father came up with a solution. He found a local tractor operator with a tractor from the kolkhoz. It had a little wooden cabin on a sled attached to the tractor by a chain. He begged him to take us to the next village thirty kilometers away. The tractor could go in the deep snow. It had caterpillar tracks, and it would move about three kilometers an hour. We wore short quilted jackets, and fur hats all made by my father, and our felt boots, which were made by a special boot maker. My father thought that we were ready to make the journey.

We started in the early evening, and by the middle of the night, we found ourselves in the center of a huge open field. It was covered in deep snow. There was nothing around, no light, not even a single tree. The temperature was dropping quickly. It was around 45 degrees below zero. Then the worst possible thing happened; the tractor broke down. It just stopped completely. My father was horrified. We could all freeze to death if we did not find a warm place soon. My father was faced with the possibility that he might lose his whole family and his own life. He made the decision to go into the night with hopes of finding people and help. It was a heroic decision. The cold, open field was full of hungry wolves He took a box of matches and a few keys with him. Wolves are afraid of fire and don't like the sound of banging metal. With this equipment, he set off on his way. We were very frightened, freezing and crying. We did not know if my father would make it. My mom was holding us tight, all together, all shaking. We were alone in the empty freezing white field. It looked unreal—all white and dead in the bright moonlight, nothing for the eye to stop on. All we could hear were the howls of hungry wolves.

The night was long, and the waiting seemed endless. My poor mom was praying to G-d to save our father and bring him back to us with help. My feet already were numb and frozen. The night started to fade as did our hope for help. Suddenly, I heard a far-off jingle of bells. I told my mom this, and she thought I was hallucinating. But soon we saw two horses pulling a sled. On that sled was my dad! Oh my G-d! Who can express the feelings all of us felt in this moment! We were crying, laughing, happy, frozen—everything.

We all piled on the sled and drove to a village. The men with the horses brought us to a house. The people there were very friendly and hospitable. A woman prepared a basin of hot water in the oven and started to save my feet. I held them in the hot water for a while, and after a man rubbed them with woolen mittens until the blood started to circulate in all my toes and I could feel them again. At that time, a wounded officer was visiting his village. He came to see us and talked to my dad. He told him what was going on in the warm states. People were dying from hunger and disease. He told him to forget this idea and go back to the village we had left. Later, I thought that it was G-d's will to keep us alive and return us to the village.

Chapter 8

Back in the Kolkhoz

The head of the kolkhoz arranged a horse with sleds for us, and in a few hours, we were back in Pestravka. We still did not have a place to live. So in a few days, by begging the local authorities, my father got a transfer to another village. It was smaller and about twenty kilometers from Pestravka. It was called Lomovka. This kolkhoz was much richer than the previous one we had lived in. They had very fertile soil, which was perfect for growing grain. There were several empty houses. The occupants were probably mobilized to the army. Now we had our own house, and we were thrilled. The house had one big room and a little kitchen with a big oven that reached into the front room. This was where my brother and I would sleep in the winter. Sleeping on the oven was very warm, and we did not have to freeze anymore. Did I love that oven!

To come into the house, you went up three steps and opened the door to a little barn that was attached to the house. It was about forty to fifty square feet in size and could be used for storage. This barn was built on wooden legs with space underneath to keep chickens or different things. From the barn, you would enter the house, kind of like a foyer. We also had a long piece of land behind the house that went down to the riverbank, where we could plant vegetables. Where the land started, there was a large hole about five feet in diameter and very deep. This was our toilet for the summer. We used large pieces of grass or leaves as toilet paper. For the winter, the toilet was just behind the house because the other one was full of snow. My father would make a snow wall around the hole for privacy. We used the snow as toilet paper!

On the outskirts of the village were large pieces of land that had never been touched. We had to dig it out and plant whatever we could. There was no food other than what we grew ourselves. We were given four shovels. Spring was coming, and this was no easy task. This land was assigned for potatoes and grain. I was digging with my parents with all my strength. Digging the virgin fields was very hard, and my mom was a weak and sickly woman. Luckily, I was able to take on a larger portion of the work. This made me the "big hero." My little brother, Samuil, who was seven at the time, was digging too.

Then the kolkhoz gave us two baby sheeps, and several families gave us chickens. We had ten of them, plus a beautiful rooster. This would be our protein source. Every evening, my mom and I would check the tushes of each chicken by putting a finger in it to see if one of them would give us an egg in the morning. This was very important. We had to watch them; otherwise, the chickens would wander away and lay the eggs in grass and we could lose them. They were supposed to lay the eggs under our house in baskets. The eggs were very important for us because they were our nourishment.

My mom did all the cooking. When she had enough flour, the bread was very good. This was a very delicious meal for me in the afternoons. If I went outside with my piece of bread, all my friends would ask for a bite and of course I would share it, then I would end up hungry. When we did not have enough grain, my dad would take the grain to the mill and bring home the flour and the bran. Mom could add the bran to the flour and the skin from the peeled potatoes to make bread. This bread was tough to eat. The bran was like pieces of straw sticking out from the slice, but it was okay because other people didn't even have this. The potato peels were never discarded, they always found a place in our meals. In our village lived two families: an older couple who were hungry most of the time because they could not work and a woman with three small, hungry children. Every two days, my mom would make a food package for both families. Whatever we had, she cut some from our share and took it to them. My parents were extremely good-hearted and generous people.

Sometimes my father would bring home honey, butter, milk, or whatever he got paid with for his work for other people. After his working hours, he would sew or fix clothing and repair sewing machines, whatever people needed. With him, we were always safe. He was our rock.

We also got two beds—one for my parents and one for me. My brother slept somewhere on the floor. The beds were very narrow, similar to a twin size, with a straw mattress. In the summer, we did not need lighting, because the days were long and we were always outside. But in the winter, it got dark early. The only light we had was a little wick lamp, which gave a dim light, but we could see each other.

Chapter 9

The Fun Times

The village had its rules. Every street was about a half a mile long, and each street had its leaders. The boys from another street could not come to our street; it was forbidden territory. They could not dance or play with our girls. In the winter evenings, all the youth from our street would gather together in somebody's house. This was welcomed because every house had their loved ones in the war and everybody felt the same loneliness, so it was kind of an escape. They would often gather in our house. My mom loved it; she was very sociable and loved to sing. At these gatherings, the boys would bring their instruments, such as balalaikas or guitars, and girls would dance to Russian folk songs and sing "chastushki" (a four-line humorous carol). The necessary treats of those evenings were delicious roasted sunflower seeds. Unfortunately, we did not have better delicacies.

After school in the winter, all the kids would slide down the hills on saucer-shaped, homemade sleds. We would start making these in the fall. To do this, we would mix clay with straw and spread it around an old tin basin or basket. Then we would let it dry until the frost came. When the weather was cold enough, we put it upside down, and poured water on it and let it freeze. We added water every day until it became a thick, shiny icicle. To make it comfortable to sit on, we put straw or old fabric inside of it. All of us would slide until we were frozen. This was heaven for us.

Once a month, in the winter, we would go to the bath. The kolkhoz had a big barn where they kept the machinery for working in the fields. Close to this barn was a tiny clay bathhouse on the bank of the river, very close to the water. In the barn, the kolkhoz kept chopped wood for the bath. The bathhouse had a metal barrel with a place to light a fire underneath it. We would bring buckets of water to fill up the barrel. The fire warmed up the water. Three or four people could fit into this little tiny bath to wash themselves. We had to run outside, naked, to get a bucket of snow to cool down the hot bathwater. Soap was rationed; a family received two large bricks of soap a year. This was to clean our bodies, as well as our clothes. To wash our hair, we had to use ashes from burned wood as shampoo if the soap was used up. For us children, it was fun. In summertime, we bathed in the river.

When springtime arrived, the big event for all the children was lice hunting! The war brought us not only hunger, hard work, and hard living conditions but also a lot of lice! The whole country faced a lice invasion, and everybody had to deal with it.

In a strange coincidence, in my mother's purse were a few combs. She probably bought them right before the war as a package deal. There was a strange little comb in this set with very thin teeth coming from both sides and no handle.

The adults already knew about lice, but I had no idea about them. So how fortunate we felt when my mom took out this little comb and started to comb through my hair. I had to bend over a white piece of paper, and as the lice fell from my head, we would hunt and kill them. All the children were waiting in line to get their lice combed out. For us, it was fun. The adult women would gather together to check each other for lice and kill them.

One day, one of my friends, Maria (in Russian, she was Maynka), decided to steal the comb. It was a terrible thing for everybody, and my mother was very upset. So I took matters into my own hands. I went to Maynka and said, "Did you comb a lot of lice from your hair? I think my mom would do a better job. Let's go to her, and she will help you."

Mainka did not know what to say. I did not accuse her of stealing, so she felt comfortable admitting she did have it. She came back to my mom with me and returned the comb, and everybody was happy.

Chapter 10

Reunited with Family

In the spring of 1942, we found out my mother's older sister, Rachel, was alive! Before the war, her husband was working in the police department. They were evacuated a few days before us. Her husband was assigned to the Latvian division of the Russian army. Rachel was living near the military base. The whole time, she was wondering what had happened to her family. She turned to the Red Cross for help. One day, she got a letter telling her they had found her sister (my mother) and gave her our address. She wrote to us right away. This was a huge joy for us. She decided to come live with us because she was pregnant at the time and the military base was not a safe place to give birth to a child.

One day, as she was going to make her travel arrangements, she saw a man trying to cross a little creek. Her intuition told her to go over to see who the man was. When she got closer to him, he looked up.

It was her younger brother Sheil! This reunion was indescribable. He was wounded in the arm, and he was going to the hospital for medical attention. It turned out his arm was very badly damaged. He ended up needing a lifetime of therapy and never regained full use of it. He told her how he had ended up in the army and how he escaped the Nazis.

He ran with my grandparents and his pregnant sister, Dora, with a two-year-old girl in her hands. They ran through the forests, and they got separated from each other. Sheil caught up with the last remainder of the running army. They took him in, and soon he was fighting on the front. Dora got away as well. Somebody who was driving by in a horse and carriage saw her and took pity on this pregnant girl with a baby in her arms. They took her safely through the border with them.

Rachel again went to the Red Cross to find the whereabouts of Dora and her children. Soon she received her answer that Dora and her children were alive and living in Tatar Republic. She wrote to her that she had found our family and that she was going to live with us.

My parents and I were very happy. I loved my aunt. When the time was closer for Rachel to give birth, everybody got worried because she had previously lost a child by cesarean section. The doctor had told her that another birth would again need a cesarean section. There was no hospital near us and no doctor, but luckily there was a midwife. She was a godsend, and my aunt had a safe natural birth. She had a baby girl—Riveka.

My cousin Riveka

Now we had a bigger family. I gave them my bed and slept on the floor. About six months later, my mom's younger sister Dora wrote to us. She would be coming to stay with us. She brought her two children, a girl and a boy. The girl was three years old and mentally retarded. The boy was almost two years old. Soon after, my Uncle Sheil came to live with us too.

Now we were a family of ten people in our one-room house. my father had to think of how to arrange a place for everybody to sleep. There was an old barn door lying around the kolkhoz machinery barn that no one was using. My dad went to the head of the kolkhoz to ask for permission to use it to make a place to sleep for our new family members. He made a low bench out of it. He sewed a big sack out of burlap and put straw in it. This became a "bed." This place was assigned to Dora with her two children. Rachel had my bed, and the second bed was for my parents. My uncle was sleeping on the floor, and my brother and I slept on the oven. The sleeping places were very important. This was kind of a domain. It was your place because there were no chairs in the house. We had a bench by the table, so in the winter, you either sat on the bench to eat or you ate on your "bed." The most difficult part for my dad was to provide for the whole family. He worked very hard. My father was a very good-hearted man. He never told my mom that her family was a burden. He shared everything.

Chapter 11

Raika the Goat

One day, my father went to another village to do all kinds of odd jobs, fixing clothes and so on. He was very handy. He came home one day with a goat he had received as payment for his work. She was beautiful with long, black hair; big, gorgeous horns; a beard; and a big white star shaped mark on her forehead. We named her Raika. Right away, Raika became a member of our family. She was like a dog, going with us for walks and following us all over. Everybody knew her in the village. She was my pal. She did not allow anybody to milk her except me. My mom had to wake me early in the morning to milk her. I was always half asleep when I milked her. It seemed like she understood this. She would lick my face so gently and lovingly. I loved her too. After milking, she would go with the cows and other cattle to the pasture with the shepherd. In the evening, she would come home full of around three liters of delicious milk. We used this milk to cook a farina meal for the little children (flour with milk). There was not enough for me and my little brother, so we would wait to scrub the pot because it was so delicious. This was in the summertime.

In the winter, the cattle did not give too much milk. It was the time for them to be pregnant, and then the first few weeks, they would feed the newborns. Raika had two little goats, and they were gorgeous. When they were a few months old, we had to sell them in exchange for other food and supplies. Under Raika's long, straight hair grew beautiful taupe downlike wool, which I would comb out in spring when she did not need it to be warm. I put the wool on a spindle and made yarn. I made yarn from lamb's wool too. In my spare time, I was knitting. I made two beautiful shawls from Raika's wool. I made everybody socks, mittens, and scarves from lamb's wool. For Riveka, I knitted a beautiful hat from the rest of the wool. How thankful we were to Raika. She gave us milk, and she gave us warmth.

The Germans were advancing very fast. They went deep into Russia like a hurricane. They did not have resistance. The Russian army fled. Nobody was prepared for this war.

Stalin had made a pact with Hitler just before the war. They would not attack each other. But this Nazi had his plans already made. He disoriented Stalin, and Stalin believed that his borders were safe. But this was not the reality. Hitler cheated him and won in tactics, and the Nazis went in like a swarm of vultures. By the end of 1942, they were nearing Kuibishev. The city was 120 kilometers from our village. All the men in our village were mobilized in the beginning of the war, and now there was a need for more soldiers. When the Germans came close to Moscow, Hitler was already planning his parade along the Kremlin wall in the Red Square. But Russia started to fight back, and the patriotism was growing. People heard about all the atrocities the Nazis had committed against the Jewish people and others. The anger grew. There were many partisan groups in the forests. The women were working in the big factories, making weapons day and night. When the Germans came to Stalingrad, the city on the Volga River (as was Kuibishev), the army was already organized. The winter of 1943 was very cold. The Germans did not have warm clothes! They were not prepared for our winter. But the Russian army was prepared for the cold weather and got much stronger. They were able to push the Germans back from the city, Stalingrad. But the war was still on full blast. The army needed food, warm clothes, weapons, and soldiers more and more.

As spring approached, the first thing we had to do was take care of our vegetable gardens. We planted tomatoes, cabbage, and cucumbers. This was our garden on the bank of the River Teplaya. We thanked G-d for this river because the garden had to be watered every day. The soil was clay and required a lot of water as well. In the backyard, we grew peapods and pumpkin plants. Behind the village was where we grew the potatoes and grain. This was the land we had already dug up. About five kilometers from the village, by a small forest, we had a place to plant watermelons and melons. Unfortunately, we did not have the strength to keep digging, so we only had a small area of melons and watermelons to plant. They were sweet like honey, but we did not have a lot of them. When we did have them, we ate them as our dinner with a piece of bread.

Besides working in our own garden, I was helping other peasants too, like my neighbor, an older woman, whose husband and sons were on the front. I milked her cow when she was sick, I weeded her garden, and I grabbed straw from the grain crops.

When the grain crops were ready to harvest, we would cut them off with a sickle. I was very good with it. We would bind them into bundles and then put them on the big buggies with the ox and bring them into the yard. We would clean the yard first with a broom and then spread out large pieces of linen that were sewn together. We put the whole harvest on it. Then with long, heavy chains, we beat the straw bundles until all the grains from the straw ears came out. We put the grain in sacks to be put away for winter.

After that, we would pick up the straw, get more straw from the kolkhoz, and make kizaki. We mixed the straw with cow manure and water. The mixing of the manure with the straw was done with bare feet, walking in the manure in circles for hours. After mixing, we made a thick layer on the ground and was then cut into squares and left to dry through the fall.

When it was dry, we put it in the barn like bricks, one on the other. It was used to heat the ovens for cooking and heating the house. It held the heat in the oven for a very long time. It burned very slowly and did not leave much ash. All the children would participate in this mixing process because there was so much to do, and would go to each house to help. For my help I often would get milk or eggs or dinner which I always divided in three parts to bring two parts home for my mom and my brother Samuil.

My family did not have cows, so we had no manure to make kizaki. I tried to bring home any piece of dry manure I could find to make even a little bit of kizaki. We still had to find another source. My dad got permission to go into the forest and saw down the dry trees. He collected the dry wood in an ox buggy and brought it back to the house. The region where we lived did not have a lot of forests. The forests that were there were protected by the government. You could only take the dried-out trees with permission from the kolkhoz.

I would go outside the village to look for tall weeds for use in the oven. I took a hatchet and chopped weeds every day for more than a week. Then I took from the kolkhoz, an ox with a buggy to load up the chopped weeds and bring it home. I worked very hard and never complained. I took pride in everything I did. This was an addition to the wood we had, and it helped to keep the house warm.

On our street, there were a few families who only had the mother at home. The fathers and older brothers were in the war. There was always a shortage of food for us. We were always trying to find new ways of getting more food, such as being on the lookout if someone died in the village. After the burial, they always served food, like vegetable soup with little pieces of meat and cookies without sugar. To us, they were delicious. We stood around with sad faces until an adult saw us and invited us in to eat. We were trained well, like little actors!

On Easter, all of the children went door to door saying, "Jesus was resurrected!" We would kiss everybody, and they would give us hard-boiled eggs and cookies. This was the custom. We used it well.

As we got closer to spring, there was little food left. It was a difficult time for everybody. But the grass started to grow, the cows had fresh food, and they started to give more milk. The chickens started to produce eggs, and life became easier. In the early summer months, we were often going to the pasture where there was a lot of edible grass, wild flowers that had edible parts, little mushrooms that could be cooked. We had a little lake that there was abundance of cattails growing. We found out that the roots inside had some edible kind of flour that we ate. So, before the vegetables were ready to be eaten, we used those wild "goodies".

Our little River Teplaya had some fish. My dad had a fishing net, so my mom and I decided to use it. The river was almost as wide as the net. Every evening, I would tie the net on our side of the river and then swim across with the net in my hand to tie up the other side. The fish could go right into the net. Early in the morning, my mom would wake me up to go to the river. I would jump in the cold water, swim to the other side, untie the net, and drag it back with the fish. Sometimes it was so heavy that I thought I might drown, but I held on tightly with my little hands and brought the fish to my mom on the riverbank. She was happily collecting the fish in a bucket. There were no refrigerators, so the fish could not keep for more than a day or two. We would trade it for other foods if we had more than we needed. The smaller fish I would salt and then lay out on the roof to dry. The dried fish made a nice snack and lasted longer than fresh fish.

Harvest time meant working hard from early morning until late at night. The pumpkins were very big and heavy and had to go under the beds. The potatoes went into the cellar. (The entrance to the cellar was in the middle of the room under the floor.) These were the most important foods. The cabbage, cucumbers, and tomatoes were pickled in a barrel. We did not have too many carrots, cucumbers, and tomatoes left because we ate them through the summer. The few watermelons that were left from the summer, we cut up into thick wedges and put them in the barrels with the cabbage mix. In the winter, that watermelon was a treat!

Once every six months, we got a bottle of syrup from the kolkhoz. Sugar was not even a word in our vocabulary! When we received the syrup, we put it on sauerkraut and ate it with bread. Sometimes, when my mom was baking bread, she would take a bit of the dough and make pirogi. They were filled with baked pumpkin and mashed potatoes. This was a very special treat for us.

After we finished our harvest, we had to go work in the kolkhoz fields because there were not enough people, as all the men were deployed. We all worked hard, including the children. We all understood how important it was to get a big harvest. We would have to get as much out of the fields as possible, so we would have enough for the people of the kolkhoz and to be able to send food to the cities and to the army. That was mandatory.

Even though every family had their own garden, it was still not enough food to get through the winter, especially in bigger families. For our work, we got paid a little portion of the grain and some potatoes. The children's job was working in the potato fields. We would follow behind the hoe, which was pulled by a bull or special machine. We collected the potatoes that came up, put them in buckets, and took them to the carts. The full carts were then taken to the storage area.

Everybody liked to work on the potato field for a very special reason—it was the easiest to steal from! By the end of the day, I could hardly walk from taking the largest potatoes and putting them in the pockets of my jacket. But my jacket was small and I couldn't carry that much. Both of my aunts always brought more. One day, I decided to bring as much as possible. I put on a pair of long quilted pants and a big jacket with a lining that

I opened up on one side. When the jacket was full, I looked like a little barrel and could hardly bend down to get more. Then I started to put the potatoes in my pants. By the time we had to go home, I looked like a big stuffed animal. I could hardly move, so my partners said that I could not go home the usual way because the managers would see me. This was a crime, and my family could be punished. So I had to go through the fields with my arms and legs spread apart. It is a shame we did not have a camera to take a picture of me. When I came home, it was dark and my mom was very worried. When my mom saw me, she could not figure out what was going on. She started to cry out for help. She thought I was paralyzed. But when I lowered my pants and opened the jacket, potatoes started falling out. She was hysterical from laughter. They were all practically peeing in their pants. I wanted to help provide for my family and show my strengths any way I could.

In spring of 1944 my Aunt Rachel was going to leave us. Her husband was wounded in his eye. He was demobilized, and sent to the city of Yeysk, where he held the post of Commandant of the city. The city was an important air force base and school. Of course he wanted his family to stay with him. My uncle Sheil went with them. This is where he would meet his future wife.

My mom's brother Sheil Barkin and his wife, Pesya

After a short time my aunt Dora left to be reunited with her husband.

So now our family was alone.

Summers were always wonderful. All the children of the village were working hard, but we were never tired. We all had a free spirit, not thinking about what was going on in the world. At night, we were organizing gangs and attacking the neighbors' gardens, stealing tomatoes and cucumbers if they were ripe before ours. But we did it for fun and adventure. We were still 11 –12 year old children.

Every fall, my two friends and I went to pick sunflower seeds. Sunflowers were used for oil and for food. The sunflower fields were closely guarded, so we had to sneak in. We took string and hung a sack around our necks. We looked for the biggest and ripest flower heads, bent them over right to the sack, and beat them with a stick until all the seeds fell out. We then let go of the head, and it snapped back into place like nothing had happened. We would not return home until the bag was full. For a week, we would collect enough seeds for the winter. Mom roasted them in the oven, and it was the best wintertime snack.

In summer 1944, it came the time for my father to be mobilized. It was a disaster for us. My mom was the most helpless housewife. She was often sick and weak. She was shy, and she always depended on my dad. My brother was only eight years old, and I was twelve and had to be in charge of the family!

The day my father was taken to the army was like a mourning day for us. We all understood that we could not survive on our own. In those days, I grew up very fast. I had to become an adult. I was the head of a helpless family. I was praying every day to G-d, begging him to send my Dad home.

Chapter 12

The Sorceress and the Gypsies

O ne day, I got up and saw my mother lying on the bed. Her face was red and swollen. I was very scared. I did not know what to do. Toward the evening, she got worse. The swelling closed her eyes, and her face was dark red and burning like a fire. She had a very high temperature.

I ran to the midwife, who was the closest thing we had to a doctor in our village. She came right away. When she saw my mom, she knew she could not help her. It was erysipelas, a bacterial skin infection. There was no cure. I was desperate. I had to save my mom. I begged the midwife to do something, anything! Otherwise, two little children would be left alone to die from hunger and cold. She sat down, got very serious, and started thinking. After a long time, she said, "There is a sorceress who lives in our village. You have to run to her."

I ran like the wind. In ten minutes, I was at her door and told her what had happened. She heard me out and then told me to go home and come back in the early morning. She said, "Do not tell anybody anything. Do not talk at all."

Early the next morning, I ran to her house. She was in a little room whispering something to her religious icons by a little oil lamp. After a while, she came out with a very small bottle of liquid and gave it to me. She said, "Run home as fast as you can. Don't stop. Don't talk to anybody, not one word. When you get home to your mother, wet her face with a little bit from the bottle, and then repeat it in the evening and again the next morning."

I believed every word she said and ran home with hope in my heart. I did not stop. I did not answer any of my friends' questions when they saw me running. I ran into the house, and right away, I poured a little of the liquid on my mom's face and spread it all over. Her face already looked like a dark-red pillow. It was burning hot and so swollen you could not see her eyes or even make out her nose. I sat by her bed the whole day, looking for improvement. I was desperate! Toward the evening, the swelling started to go down a little bit. I could see little slits of her eyes. Her temperature went down too. I wet her face with the "medicine" again. I did not sleep the whole night. I watched as my mom was getting better and better.

By the evening of the second day, she was already sitting up in bed, talking. The swelling was almost gone! Oh G-d! It was a miracle! My mother was saved! If only my father could be with us to see it!

One day, I went to the well for water. This was my first job, to provide fresh water for my family for cooking and drinking. It was a half mile away, and it was the only well on our street. I carried a yoke with two buckets full of water and one in my hand—three buckets. On the way home, I met a group of gypsies. They were hunted by the Nazis too.

They came to our village, moving from one village to the other to find food. It was a big event for us children. They read their strange cards telling our fortunes. At night, we all ran to the outskirts of our village where the gypsies placed their tents. They lit a big fire and sat around, singing their gypsy songs and dancing. It was fun for the children. We were charmed by the uniqueness of these people.

The next day, they were going house to house, offering their knowledge of fortune-telling with cards, little strange books, and the palm of your hand in exchange for an egg, a piece of bread, or whatever. When a gypsy came to our house, I was very excited. I wanted to know our fortune. We missed our dad terribly. So I begged my mom to let the gypsy read her palm, cards, and book. She did not want to at first, but I was persistent and she gave in. That was when the magic started. She told her that she had three sisters;

their names were not very clear but close. The gypsy told her she had two brothers and that her man was in the army but she should not worry.

"Seven nights will pass, and in the middle of the eighth night, there will be a light knock on the window," she said. "This would be your man (my father) and he would have a sack of dried bread."

My mom did not believe them, and she was sorry that she had let them read her fortune. She was very disturbed. But I believed every word they said, and it gave me high hopes. I was counting the days patiently and secretly. On the eighth night, I did not go to sleep. I was waiting for my dad. Mom was scolding me for believing in nonsense and saying it would never happen. We hadn't heard a word from him in three months. She said I should just go to sleep. I think she probably counted the days secretly too but did not want to admit it because the disappointment would be too hurtful. I lay down on my straw mattress, fighting the sleepiness that came over me, but nature took over and I fell asleep. Even in my sleep though, I was very alert. I woke up from a light knock on the window. In a second, I was outside hugging my dear father. The gypsies did not lie! Oh, what a happy family was standing under the moonlight on the street! We were safe now!

My brother did not understand what would happen to us without our father. He was happy because he missed him very much. Life got easier and happier. I was my dad's right hand, helping him with everything. He started to work again in the tailor shop for the army, and in our free time, I was going fishing with him or quail hunting, so we could have more food. We got a little pig. We called him Boris. He was given to us by the collective farm to provide us with meat in the winter. But Boris quickly became a member of our family, even though he was a big troublemaker. He would run into the house and turn everything upside down in the kitchen—including the buckets of water and the garbage. It was a mess, but we loved him very much anyway. I started to take him to the fields behind the village. There, he could eat fresh grass and run around like crazy. He was always running around very fast, and I had to chase after him. He really gave me a run! When the winter came, we had to slaughter him. We were all so upset we were crying. It was terrible. We did not want to eat his meat, but hunger forced us and we had to—not my mother. She refused to eat his meat.

In late summer of 1944, the war was going farther and farther from our village. The fascists were getting beaten from two fronts: America and Russia. America was finally involved in the war, and we hoped that soon the monster would be extinct.

One morning, I woke up with a strange feeling like I was very ill. My little "dots" (nipples) where the breasts were supposed to be were painful and swollen. I ran to my father, crying, that I was so ill and I am going to die. I showed him what had happened—the hard, swollen bubbles. I insisted that he should touch them to see for himself how bad it was. Dad hesitated for a moment and then very gently touched them. With a gentle, shy smile, he explained to me that I was growing up and everything grew with me.

"There is nothing to be afraid of. It is normal. Just be careful, and it will heal."

In a few months, the "bubbles" started to grow bigger and the pain decreased and finally was gone. I couldn't run around without a shirt anymore or just in crazy looking underwear. This was the only clothing I had for summer! The clothing situation was very bad— no shoes, no dress, no material even to make a dress. Dad cut up my old dress that I wore at the beginning of the war and some old remnants of uniforms and made me something resembling a dress. In the winter, I wore a quilted jacket, quilted pants, fur hat, and felt boots made by an old man in the village. Now I was trying to walk more gracefully with my chest pushing forward. I was very proud of my changes.

As it happened, all the girls were the same or close in age, and we could see each other's changes. We measured who had bigger boobs. All of a sudden, the boys were growing up too and they started to notice our changes. We were not just a bunch of kids anymore. They started to favor one girl more than the others and show off. Changes were on the way. They became dominating and were chasing us to catch and squeeze unmercifully our small, still very sensitive breasts. This was a custom in the village, and thirteen-year-old boys do not have much sense. This was their way of showing that they liked the girl. And we had to suffer and be quiet, not showing our bitter, painful tears because we had to be proud of the attention we were getting. We laughed with all of them, not showing anything—bastards!

Chapter 13

The Victory

I finished sixth grade. I was a straight-A student. I had a phenomenal memory. I could repeat word for word everything the teacher would say, and when he was asking questions on a subject, I was the first to answer. In our class, we had another A student, Nikolay Komarov. He was very strong in math. So school for me was very easy.

In the sixth grade, we already had to pass exams on every subject. To the exams, we always brought flowers for the teachers and wore the best clothes we had. I did not have clothes, so my mom took out her beautiful silk dress that she had brought from home all those years ago, keeping it for the day to come, and gave it to me to wear. But it did not look good with bare feet, so she gave me her shoes from home. They were high heels. Since I was always going barefoot, my feet had grown pretty big, and my mom's size 5 shoes were too tight on me. I could hardly put them on. I went to school so dressed up and so proud, but it looked like I was going on crutches. During the exam, my feet felt like they are on fire. I had to take the shoes off. I passed my exam with no shoes. I did very well. I went home with the shoes in my hands, gave them to my mom, and asked her never to give me those shoes again.

We did not have radios in the houses. The only one was in the village hall. There was a loudspeaker on the small square, and all of a sudden, we heard, "Attention! Attention!"

We all ran to the square. Soon the whole village was there, and the loudspeaker was yelling, "Victory! Victory! The enemy is beaten! The war is finished!" Those were unforgettable words. It was May 9, 1945.

Everybody cried out the word *victory*. We were staying in the little square, hugging each other, laughing and crying, crying for those sons, brothers, fathers, and husbands who would never come home. We were listening to Stalin's speech about the victory, about the heroes who made it, the heroes who fell for it, and the women who gave all their strength to work day and night to support the army.

The evening was very lively. The village did not sleep. The young people—the oldest were sixteen to seventeen years old—were singing war songs and dancing in the streets.

I could not fall asleep. I was dreaming about going home, seeing my dearest grandparents, uncles, and aunts. I dreamed that I would have a nice dress, a real one, a nightgown, real underwear, a coat, and shoes, which I did not have the whole time—four years.

One night, there was a very big rain and thunderstorm. My brother and I were sleeping on the floor under a window. We did not have extra blankets, so we slept together to have one piece of material to cover us, and on the oven was too hot. I woke up at a very strong thunderclap. The lightning had struck the tree by the window and probably went a little bit through me because I was all trembling from fear and shaking. My teeth clacked and crunched together so tight that I could not talk. I became very ill. A whole week, I lay in bed; I could not move my legs or hands.

One day, I tried to get up. The reaction was terrible. I started to feel like I was dying. I told my mom that I was dying. My poor mom got so scared that she turned over a bucket of water to do something. It was an awful experience. From an energetic, full-of-life girl, I had turned into a weak, sick invalid, hardly walking, crying at everything, and sitting all day on the doorstep of our house. I could not run around with my friends anymore. It was very upsetting.

My father started to bustle about going back home. He went to Kuybishev to get a permit to go home. Everything was strictly done with permits. For me to go to the city was a dream. In our village, nobody was ever in a big city. The city seemed a world away.

When my dad returned, he brought me a dress, which was white with yellow flowers, and the best thing—a pair of slippers, real leather shoes. They were hard like a rock. It was painful to walk in them, but they were real shoes and we were going home!

Now we had to decide what to do with Raika. We were very picky about whom to sell her to. We were looking for good people who would be good to her. We were sorry that we could not take her with us. Dad sold her to a good woman. But Raika ran away from the new owner three times. And every time, we had to drag her back. When we were loading ourselves onto the truck that was taking us to Kuybishev, all of a sudden, we saw our dear Raika, running after the truck. We were all crying. She loved us. She had a heart full of love and felt our love for her. The day we had to part with her, it was like mourning a close friend. I will never forget Raika.

Chapter 14

Life after War

H ome! How exciting! I left home a little innocent, gentle girl who wanted to watch the war through the window, pampered, loved, and cared for in a lovely home. I went every summer to a resort by the lake and forest. I was always beautifully dressed and a good pianist with a promising future. Now I was returning a teenager who had gone through a hard life, working like a grown-up, seeing hunger, cold, and fright. But I considered myself lucky, because six million of my people did not make it to this day. They were slaughtered in the ghettos, gas chambers, or buried alive in mass graves, that they were made to dig themselves.

What would we return to?

In 1945, Latvia was still a forbidden zone for people to travel to or visit. The war was over, but a lot of Latvian fascists were hiding in the forests, terrorizing and killing people, even though there was still a curfew.

Police and military groups conducted raids into the woods to catch them, jail them, and have justice done.

Our city was about 75 percent ruined. There were very few buildings left, and they were already occupied. Even the little stores along the streets were occupied by the returning refugees. We came later than other people, and we couldn't get our apartment back. It was occupied by other people. We went to our hometown, and we did not have a place to stay! We were staying in the middle of the street. We didn't have one door to open nor a roof over our heads to sleep under. We did not even have luggage. All we had was our two pillows that we had made from the four little ones and a twin-size down blanket that Dad had bought in Kuybishev. He purchased it just before we took the train to go home. He was thinking probably that it was almost fall and we had nothing to cover up with. We were devastated. There was no place to go! It was already evening, and my father decided to go from door to door to ask if somebody would let us in for the night.

At one of the little stores on the street, my father all of a sudden came to a door and the man who opened the door turned out to be our good acquaintance with whom we had lived in Pestravka. He was a photographer there, and he did the same thing in this little store. He let us in and offered the floor in the front room. The back room was where he was staying with his family—two daughters and a son. This was Mr. Blair. His children were sleeping on the floor too in one corner. We took the other corner. Mom put the pillows on the floor, and we covered up with our blanket, which we laid sidewise. It was short and not enough anyway, but it was still a blanket. Thank G-d we had somewhere to sleep. My dad was hoping that in the morning he would go to the city hall and get a room to live in. But it turned out that it was not an overnight stay. My father looked for a place for us for three or four days. Nothing was available. He was spending days in the city hall, begging the officials to find something.

One day, my father came back with a happy face. We got a room in a four-bedroom apartment. Each room was filled with a family. The room was on the third floor, and it had a balcony from which you could see the whole main street. This was an asset. A rich family had lived in this apartment before the war, and this room was very nice. We got a beautiful room, but it was completely empty—no chair, no table—but we were happy. We had our two pillows and the blanket. We could sit on them and eat on the floor. It was already September.

For five to six weeks, we were sleeping on the bare floor, lying very close to each other, trying to stretch the blanket to each side. Our feet stuck out anyway, so we were sleeping in socks and shoes. We could not take off our clothes. It was very cold. Latvia is a northern country, and September was already very cold. By November, winter was already in full blast. We did not have wood to heat the oven. We could not stay in this room any longer. In the meantime, my mother's sister

Rachel got a room in a two-bedroom apartment. She asked us to move in with them, and we did.

The apartment had one bedroom, one dining room, and a small kitchen. The bedroom was occupied, so we all had the dining room—107 square feet for nine people. There were our two families and my cousin. She did not have any surviving close family and had no place to live, so she came to live with us. It was a room with no furniture, but it was on the first floor. That made it easy to bring in wood to light the oven for warmth.

At that time, a few of the native people came to my father and told him about Willis, the policeman who had hated me so much. As soon as the Germans came, he ran to our apartment and took all of our furniture and all our belongings, including my piano. Now his family lived on a farm not far from the city.

My father went to the police to ask for a guard, a truck, and permission to go to the farm. When my father came back a few hours later, he came with a full truck of our furniture, including the armoire and mirror, a little cabinet for food and dishes, two beds, and our round table with chairs. The very best item of all was my piano. It was impossible to describe our happiness. Yes, it was very crowded with nine people, but it was warm and a place to live, eat, and sleep. The better furniture they had taken was not there. They probably sold it.

Willis was hiding, along with the other Nazis, in the forests around the city. My uncle was working in the police force at the time. He organized a group of military and special forces men to hunt for the killers.

It took about a month to locate the killers and force them out of the forest. Many of them were shot. The rest were brought to justice and jailed. This was a relief to all of us because they were all armed and dangerous.

My father started to work right away because we had to eat, and food could be obtained only with ration cards. He went to a tailor shop, where mostly was made cloth for the military. You couldn't buy fabric anywhere, and I was completely without clothes. One day, he brought me a dress that he had made himself from a half burned pilot's jacket. There was not enough material for it, so a big burned-out hole was in the middle of the bottom of my dress just in the front. I was very embarrassed to wear it, but it was warm and I did not have another one, so there was no choice. That was how I came one day in September in the seventh grade. It was difficult to get used to the hole in the front of my dress. I sat in the class when it was recess, going only to the toilet. I would go into the classroom sidewise, holding a notebook in the front.

I looked like a crippled little creature. I was very small and very thin with a big head of golden curls. My health was not good. The lightning shock's effects did not pass. Almost every day, I had an anxiety attack, scaring my parents by telling them that I was dying. No medicine helped. The doctors said that we had to wait for my periods to come. I also lost my phenomenal memory. It was never the same after this.

It was coming up to November 7, a holiday, the day of the October revolution. In school, there was going to be a big event with a concert and dance and some treats—a piece of bread with sugar on top. Who would want to miss all this? But I could not go because I had nothing to wear. I could not go to a such big ball with a notebook in front of the hole. I was very upset and sad. My parents were frustrated because it was my first party in a normal school. I could hardly keep myself from crying. I did not want to upset my parents even more. It was a difficult time for everybody. The whole country was hungry and naked. The United States was helping with food and clothes. These necessities were given to the people by ration and according to who needed them more. But like everywhere, corruption was rampant. Whoever was closer to the source, got more.

Before the big event, some presents were coming to the kids in school. My class received three vouchers for clothes, and they were given to the neediest in the class. And sure enough, all the teachers voted for me too. They saw my suffering. My excitement and happiness were incredible. I could not wait to go home and run to the store where my ticket would be exchanged for a dress. Dad was not home, and I did not have the patience to wait until he came home, so I ran by myself to the store. I was very shy, but the ticket in my hands gave me strength. I proudly presented it to a salesgirl.

The salesgirls were very indifferent and did not care who was needy. They cared only who would pay them under the table. I did not know that you could get a better piece of cloth. All the good stuff was stashed away, and cloth that nobody needed was in the front. When I saw what I was getting, all my rainbow dreams faded away, my eyes were full of tears, and I hardly saw my way home. I got a tiny little skirt for a doll, or maybe it would fit a one-year-old. The girl who gave me the skirt later became my sister-in-law Rosa.

It was the darkest and most unforgettable day of my childhood. But God was with me and miracles do happen.

A day before the party, my father came home early, holding a package in his hands. He told me to take off my dress and handed me a beautiful burgundy silk dress in a gorgeous style—something I could not even dream about. In a second, it was on me, and it fit perfectly, like it was made for me. I felt like Cinderella. I could not believe my eyes. When my excitement cooled down, my father took out two more beautiful dresses. This was already overwhelming! I felt like a princess with three beautiful new dresses!

The dresses Dad got for me were from an officer who came to him to make up a suit. The officer came from Germany with a big suitcase full of clothing. My dad saw the dresses in the suitcase and begged the man to give him a few for his daughter, which he did. I was on cloud nine. I went to my school party, proudly wearing my beautiful dress. I ate my delicious bread with sugar on top and even danced a few times. I was noticed as a person, and my life got better.

When I finished seventh grade, my father said that it was time to start playing piano again. I was enrolled in our city's music school.

When one does not play for over five years, no matter if one is a child or an adult, one can forget everything, mostly one's technique. In the beginning, this was what it was like for me. But it didn't take long for me to get back to my music. I progressed very well, and my teacher, Mrs. Fridland, was very proud of me. She told me I had a bright future ahead, and the next step was to play concerts. This was very bad news for me. After being struck by lightning during the storm a year or so before, I was very nervous. This resulted in terrible stage fright, which continued throughout my life. When I had to come out and play, my mother stayed nearby with tranquilizer drops to help calm me down. It did not help. I was shaking like a leaf. I could barely see what I was doing. I felt like I was playing in a fog. I don't even know how I did it. It was like torture for me. But my teacher and the principal of the school were determined to make me play. They said I was the pride of the school, and they dreamed of having a talented pianist come out of their school.

I did not know what to do. I tried very hard, but finally, with a broken heart, I had to tell my father I could no longer play. He dreamed of me becoming a famous pianist and seeing me play concerts. But I just could not do it. The stage became a frightening place for me. I could not get over it. It was very sad for me to have to quit my music. My parents were very upset.

So my dreams did not come true. Even when I got much older and I attended piano concerts, I would always cry, thinking it could have been me.

In our apartment, the second bedroom was occupied by a young woman named Agnes. She was plump with a very round face and long eyebrows, almost down to her cheekbones. She was always smiling and showing the gap between her front teeth. She was a good-natured woman and worked at the restaurant bar at the railroad station. It was a very good job, liquor was very scarce at this time and was not available to purchase by the public. It was only available in restaurants. So Agnes would sell it under the table at a high price or would cheat the customers by serving them smaller amounts.

Everything in Russia was rationed. Anyone who had access to food, liquor, or clothing was most likely cheating or stealing. It was the only way to make a decent living because the wages were very low and not enough to live on. This lack of domestic goods made these types of activities part of normal life in Russia. They had revisions to check all the workers, but the revisioners were paid off too. Everybody had to make a living.

Agnes would often bring one of these revisioners home with her at night. Because vodka was very much in demand and in limited quantities, she was checked every week at work. She was checked on how much vodka was sold, if the money balanced with the sales, and whatever was left over. It was not easy to meet all this. Agnes would pay them off by giving them food and drinks and inviting them home to sleep with her. This was her lifestyle.

We lived in the first room, and the door from the corridor opened right into our room. Agnes had to go through our room to get to her room. She lived alone in her room. In our room, one wall had two windows, and one wall had the door to Agnes's room and the door to the kitchen.

We had two walls where we lined up two beds on one side and a bed and a small sofa and armoire on the other. In between, we had a dining room table. The beds were all twin size. My parents, aunt, uncle, and cousin and I got the beds. My brother slept on the sofa, and my aunt's two children, Riveka and Abram, who was born on May 1946, slept on the floor under the table because was not possible to get a crib. I had to sleep with my cousin. This was very bothersome to me and my parents because she was big and heavy and I was little and thin. We slept on opposite sides, but in the morning, my father would have to pull me out from under her heavy leg. I was getting no rest at all. It was like a punishment for me, and it upset my parents very much.

Then in the middle of the night, Agnes would come home with her next revisioner, passing through the whole room, stumbling around, drunk, waking everyone up. My father was very worried that one day he would find me choked under one of my cousin's legs. So he begged Agnes to let me sleep in her bedroom on a little couch. Our apartment was long and narrow, and the little couch was across from her bed. She could almost reach me from her bed! But it was okay because I was finally saved from my cousin and got to sleep alone, enjoying every minute of my privacy. But it was not for long.

One night, Agnes came home as usual with her next revisioner. I was sleeping. In the middle of the night, I woke up because of a strange noise. It was heavy breathing and moaning. I opened my eyes, and in the darkness, I saw Agnes on her bed, on all fours, and a man working very hard on her from behind. I did not understand right away what was going on. I thought he was going to kill her. Then, all of a sudden, she started laughing, and I understood she was playing with him. I was seeing something I had never seen and didn't know much about. I got so scared I started to shake. I could not sleep anymore. This was the last time I slept in her room. I told my father I was afraid of the men and could not sleep there anymore. Soon Agnes got a better room in another apartment, and we got the second room for us, for our two families. We were very lucky!

My aunt Rachel, with her family, moved into Agnes's room. Now we had a two-room apartment for ourselves.

We had a kitchen with a large wood-burning stove and a very tiny sink with a faucet that only had icy-cold water. Every morning, we would wait in line to wash our faces and brush our teeth. My brother hated the cold water. He did not want to wash his face. We had an argument every morning. To wash our bodies, we went to the public bath once a week.

My brother Samuil Zikherman,
1956-1957 in the Navy

Our toilet was cold and dimly lit. It was an old building. On the right side of the wall, we hammered in a large nail in the wall to put our "toilet paper" on. This was old newspapers that were cut into squares and hung on the nail. Newspapers became a desirable luxury for everybody. Because real toilet paper was unknown, whenever someone saw a newspaper, he or she would take it or steal it. Our hands were always black from handling the newspapers. I can't imagine what our tushes looked like! I never thought about it, because it was our way of life.

One day, something happened to me. I ran out from the bathroom, screaming, "Mother, I cut myself with the paper! My bottom is bloody! Oh G-d, what did I do?" It was just a piece of old newspaper.

My mother was smiling at me, calming me down and saying, "It is nothing dangerous. It means you are growing up and becoming a young lady. I will cut up an old pillowcase for you to use, to keep yourself clean."

It was not easy to walk around with a piece of pillowcase between my legs, holding it in place. It would move around to my back or belly. I had to wash it every day, and I could not stand it. So my mom asked my father to bring home some pieces of cotton that were used for stuffing the lining of winter parkas. It was dark gray, and I hated it. My mom had the idea to go to the pharmacy to get some white medicinal cotton. The pharmacy worker was an acquaintance of my mom's, so she obliged. She could only provide us with this cotton a few times. It was a prescription-only item. Soon after, we were able to get a prescription from a doctor. It was a nuisance every month. The government did not do anything to help with any women's health issues until the Soviet Union fell apart. It was only then we were introduced to new ways of dealing with women's issues like these.

At this point, I was in the eighth grade, junior high. Life started to normalize and school was a lot of fun.

In the ninth grade, I was elected head of the class until graduation. Our class had 16 boys and 14 girls. We all became close friends and did everything together. We were like a big family. We did good and bad together, we helped each other get better marks, but we also helped each other get into trouble too!

If we decided to run away from a boring lesson, the boys would put a wet piece of paper under the electric bulb. This would cause the electricity to be knocked out for an hour or two. So we ran out to the movies! The next day, I was called to the principal's office. I was "interrogated" as to who did this, but "I never knew".

All the holidays, we celebrated together in someone's apartment, preparing nice foods, and dancing to records. Every year, we had exams for every subject. It took a whole month to go through all the exams. After the exams, we celebrated by riding bikes to the park for picnics and having the best time. We had to prepare for our own graduation ball by collecting money. The principle allowed us to sell tickets to a Saturday night dance party for the public. We had our own orchestra. My friend Alexander played the accordion, another boy played the drums, and I played the piano. It worked out pretty good. We collected a lot of money. We made ourselves the best graduation ball ever in the school. My mom cooked the best dinner, and we hired an orchestra. It was the best evening. We were all saying good bye to each other, hugging and promising to stay in touch. We all ended up going to different colleges, so it was very sad.

In the meantime, my cousin got married and moved out. She married a man she did not love, but he had his own house.

Since this occurred, our living conditions had improved, now that we had the whole apartment to ourselves. My aunt's children no longer slept under the table. They had their room with their parents. They got two portable beds. We had one bed less in our room, so it was easier to breathe.

Life was getting easier. On the black market, we could buy bread, socks, material to sew clothing, and so on. My father found a shoemaker who was working out of his house. He made me a pair of shoes. I cannot say they were the best fit for me, and they were pretty hard leather, but they looked nice. I was already used to suffering from tight shoes, so it was okay. My father sewed me a coat, and we would either buy or sew underwear and nightgowns.

My first real coat and shoes after the war. I was in 9th grade. It was still our city in ruins.

Both families lived together in this little two-room apartment for seven years until I finished high school and two years of college, from 1945 to 1952. It was crowded, but we managed very well. All my friends from school loved to come celebrate all the birthdays in our room. We would sing and dance, and my mother and aunt joined in with us. There was always a lot of happiness, laughter, joy, and music. I never felt unhappy that I had no privacy. We were living like one big, happy family, and it was the best time of my life.

The Rudashevski Family- My mother's sister Rachel, her husband Israel, and children Riveka and Abram.

My mother would still look out the window to see if she could offer a bowl of soup to a person in need.

I never forgot the dear people I lost during the war. I always light a candle in their memory. On May 1 I light for my Aunt Golda and Uncle Haim. On November 7th, I light the candles for my grandparents and all the older people that were killed on this day. November 7th was the day of the Soviet revolution in Russia. The Nazis decided to have a massacre. My dearest people will live forever in my heart.

I hope history will not repeat itself. I want the next generation to remember and never allow these atrocities to happen to any nationality of people. I want people to understand that Nazism or anti-Semitism or hatred to other nations - small minorities - is a terrible thing against humanity. Human beings have to treat each other with respect and compassion. I want the young generation to learn that bad will never bring good, and only good deeds can bring goodness to the world. I also want the world to understand that Jewish people try to bring the best to our world.

Let's make the World a beautiful, peaceful, safe, and friendly place to live.

The End

My Family

Gary and Gita Greisdorf

My daughter Luba Matison

My son Jacob with his wife Robin and
their children Ryan, Jade and Elise.

My grandson Kameron Greisdorf

Aunt Dora Mirman with her sons Lazar and Mark

About the Cover

Gita at four years old with her mother's cousin,
Rachel Brez holding her on her
lap on the cottage (1935)

Printed in the United States
By Bookmasters